THE ADVENTURES

Mandy Gray

OF BUNNY AND JODY

For my Emma and Clara who bring me
countless adventures.

Special thanks to Jody Dix and Falcone Homes
for building our beautiful home.

Bunny woke one morning, **hopped** out into the sun.

He yawned and **stretched** hoping,

today he'd find some **fun**.

Jody built **houses,**

each day
working hard.

Today was
no different,
except
for the
curious
bunny in the
yard.

Bunny heard Jody working,
hammering away.

He liked the sound
and decided, he
would stay
to **play**.

Jody **noticed** Bunny,

following him around.

He didn't mind but didn't have **time**,

to **play** with the bunny on the ground.

Jody started
painting,

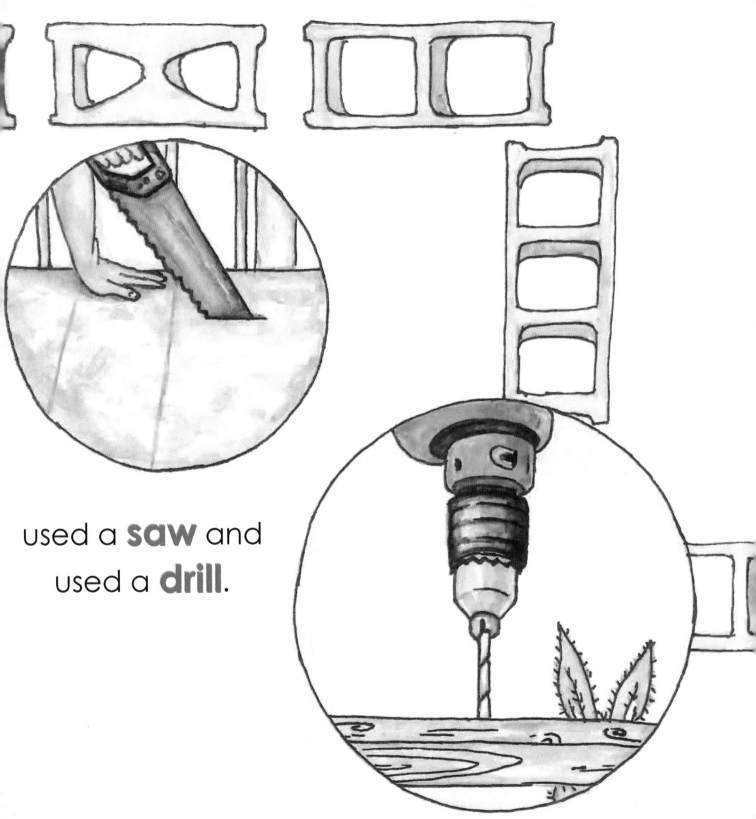

used a **saw** and
used a **drill**.

Bunny loved to watch each step,
building houses was a **thrill**!

Thinking through every **precious** step,
placing carefully each nail and screw;

Bunny saw how Jody's hard work, was helping a family's **dream** come true.

The **sun** was finally setting,
Jody's long day of work was
through; he looked
down to see that Bunny,

was now **sleeping** at his shoes.

"I'm sorry I wasn't more fun today, there's still more **work** to do...

I'm awfully **glad** you're here though, my day has been more fun with you."

Bunny **hopped** to Jody's lap, and let out a sleepy sigh.

He knew he would come back tomorrow,
and this was not **goodbye**.

Proof

31554554R00018